# Serving the Senator

L.M. Mountford

L.M. Mountford
United Kingdom
Serving the Senator

Published 2021
By The Lord of Lust Publications

Edited by readabit: Copy Editing and Proofreading Services Est 2018

L.M. Mountford – 2nd Ed.
ISBN: 978-1-913945-40-4

THE LORD OF LUST PUBLICATIONS

# ABOUT THE AUTHOR

A self-confessed Tiger fanatic, L.M. Mountford was born and raised in England, first in the town of Bridgewater, Somerset, before later moving to the city of Gloucester where he currently resides. A fully qualified and experienced Scuba Diver, he has travelled across Europe and Africa diving wrecks and seeing the wonders of the world.

# Other Titles by L.M. Mountford

## Collections
Deliciously Sinful Liaisons
Just A Number
Sweet Temptations Boxset

## The Sweet Temptations Series
The Babysitter
The Boss's Daughter

## Just Friends Series
Just Once

## Broken Heart Series
Broken

## Confessions of a Trophy Wife
Forbidden Desire

## Stand Alone Titles
Uncovered
Serving the Senator
Together in Sydney
Blood Lust
Training Tracey
Reckless
Tequila Sunset

# Don't Miss Out

Sign up for my newsletter and receive weekly updates on my writing progress, cover reveals, public appearances, reviews, and a FREE eBook.

That's right, a free book every week.

And, sometimes even chances to win advanced copies of my next book before anyone else. So, subscribe to my mailing list today, and keep up will all my new releases and special deals, exclusive to my inner circle.

Subscribe via my website

lmmountford.com

# Serving
# THE SENATOR

## Dom Diaries 4

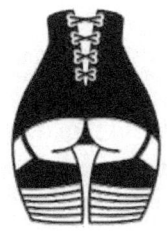

### THE LORD OF LUST
# L.M. MOUNTFORD

# Chapter One

I stand before them, bare and unadorned, a sacrificial lamb for their lusts.

My world is black, the blindfold ensuring I can't see a thing, but I can feel them. Feel them arrayed around me, their eyes raking over me, devouring me from head to toe. Making my skin shiver with gooseflesh as the heat of their eyes burns across my breasts before licking down the flat of my belly to my...

I can hear them too. Their murmurs and bawdy jokes. I know I should feel insulted. They're acting like I'm some prize stud mare they're preparing to bid on. But the game is just too exhilarating.

I'm standing before them, naked and blindfolded, waiting for their command, and I love it.

I feel **him** coming up behind me.

He doesn't say a word, doesn't make a sound, but the sensation he always sends through me when he's near ripples up my spine, sending the pit of my belly into cartwheels. Then he's right behind me. So close, I can feel **it** nestling between my buttocks. I have to force myself to stay still, my heart fluttering like a robin redbreast in a cage.

"Don't move," he orders, his voice low so only I can hear, his breath curling over the skin of my neck, making my whole-body tingle. It is a very sexy voice, as deep and cultured as a lush red wine, and authoritative. The voice of a man who gives orders all day and expects them to be obeyed.

It sends tiny shocks of ecstasy rushing straight down to the hot slickness at my centre and makes my clit greedily throb for more.

I nod my understanding, then hiss a soft gasp, more from surprise than pain, as he slaps my ass.

"Don't move," he repeats, louder this time, emphasising every word so our audience can hear. The stinging handprint he leaves on my poor butt seems to burn deliciously in answer. A part of me wants to nod again, to push him and see how far he will go, but I don't. I remain still and obedient, compliant. Submissive.

His hands come up slowly, enveloping me from behind, the tips of his fingers sliding up my belly and over my ribs to cup my breasts. I whimper at the contact. Robbed of sight, my other senses seem heightened, making my already sensitive tits deliciously tender as he rolls and tweaks my stiff nipples.

I heard him chuckle as my back curls, offering up more of my not inconsiderable cleavage. Secretly, that mischievous part of me hopes he might punish me again. Perhaps bend me over and spank me in front of all these men.

He is subtler than that. Instead, he takes his time, plumping and kneading with just the right amount of attention and neglect to work my body into a heated frenzy that has me all but chewing my lower lip.

"Such a horny girl."

His tone is hot and hungry, much like the way his cock is pushing against my butt and smearing slickness along my thighs, and I know he is enjoying this as much as I am. He enjoys teasing, being in control while pushing his paramour to the brink and watching her writhe in delirious ecstasy.

*So I writhe. Mewing soft kittenish sounds, I push back with a roll of my hips, grinding my butt along his length, the thick mushroom head sliding closer and closer to my burning cun-*

"Kora... Kora! Are you listening?"

# Chapter Two

Startled out of my thoughts, I looked up to see my supervisor standing over me, hands on her hips and watching me pointedly from behind her pearl mask.

*Oh crap...*

My belly did a triple summersault under that look. Though by no means unkind, in the few weeks I'd been working under her, Demeter had quickly set about ensuring I knew she was a woman not to be pissed about. Who would enjoy *punishing* any girl that forgot it.

*And had, frequently.*

Heat blossomed across my cheeks. I quickly nodded before looking down at my feet. "Yes Ma'am."

I always had difficulty meeting her eyes. She was just one of those women who could totally disarm you with a look and carried herself with the confidence of a woman who owned her sexuality. I was totally overwhelmed by her and couldn't help feeling totally inadequate whenever she was close. Against her cascade of lush chestnut-red curls, sharp angular features, intense blue-grey eyes and gorgeous 4"11' build that seemed made for her leather corset styled bustier, I was a plain Jane.

"*Sure.*"

I could feel her gaze scorching my skin as she eyed me, clearly not believing my less-than convincing lie, and I could just imagine her long and immaculate eyebrow arching beneath the mother of pearl likeness of her namesake. God only knows how long she might have been watching me just standing here, lost in my own little world.

My stomach flipped again, winding itself into a tight little knot. This wasn't the first time she'd caught me daydreaming. I'd been warned before, but I couldn't help myself. It was this place, it practically oozed sex appeal- as did the clientele.

*God, please don't let me get the sack...*

I needed this job. Student loans, along with my parents' debts, had left me broke. I couldn't afford getting my ass thrown back onto the job market after only a couple of weeks.

To my surprise, she just sighed and shrugged, like I was a naughty child that just wouldn't learn a simple lesson. "Go attend to the gentleman at table 12."

I couldn't believe my ears. "Ta-table...*12?*" Just saying that had the heat licking out from my centre, making my knees shake and my already slick pussy purr.

*Oh God, no! Not 12, I'm not ready for that.*

"12," she reiterated, in a tone that could cow the God of thunder. "He's waiting."

It was the epic clash of ice and fire. The cool edge to her tone crashed over the warmth in my centre.

Nodding again, I darted around her, so desperate to be out of my alcove and her sight, before she changed her mind, that I only just caught myself as I stepped out into the main smoking room. The close call earned me a hissed *tisk* from Demeter. *Graceful*, I hastily remind myself.

*A maiden of the Olympus club is always graceful, and ready to serve.*

Set amongst the heights of Midtown's numerous high-rise buildings, the Olympus Club was New York City's best kept secret. The exclusive *Gentleman*'s club of the city's elite. The den of vice and skulduggery. A house that catered to any and every pleasure. There was just one rule. Discretion.

The patron's valued their privacy and the *secrecy* the Olympus Club assured. Any member or maiden, regardless of wealth or position, status or connections, discovered discussing Olympus, would immediately be branded '*excommunicado*'.

The smoking room rang to the song of chinking of crystal, and soft girlish giggles.

It was a masculine place. The furnishings were all deep, rich, hard wood and leather. Leather so supple and deeply padded that the management liked to joke they should arrange a contest to test it against a baby's bottom and a Labrador pup's fur, just to see which was softer. Original Picasso's and Monet's, Van Gogh's, and one that looked suspiciously like a 'liberated' Da Vinci, adorned the timber panelling. However, the greatest hidden treasure was the 'trillion dollar' view overlooking the cityscape, commanding views across Times Square and all the way downtown.

It took every last ounce of my self restraint not to succumb to the lure of the floor to ceiling window that made up the smoking room's outer wall as I slid around the frolicking patrons. One little look and it was as if all of New York knelt at my feet. I dare say that was the idea. Nothing stroked the egos of the mighty more than being made to feel like gods.

If nothing else, it was a long way up from my parent's place in Washington Heights.

Dionysus, the barman, looked up at me as I approached the bar and presented me with a serving tray decorated with sterling silver filigree.

"N-number 12," I said, my voice still a little shaky at the prospect.

*God, get a grip girl, he's just a man.*

By the way he moved so expertly towards a specific bottle, I had no doubt he knew exactly what to serve each patron. Though a most impressive number of decanters and bottles stood at the ready, they were just a fraction of what the Olympus's cellar had to offer, and he filled a tumbler with scotch, adding just a single cube of ice.

If I didn't know better, I would have sworn there was just a hint of a smirk to his lips as he placed the glass on my tray. Then he returned to his station, so I put it out of my mind.

There was no point dwelling on such things. Dionysus was practically an institution at the Club, he knew all the stories, all the skeletons hidden away, and not just those figurative ones. He wouldn't say a thing, even if I called him out and asked what was so funny.

*As if I didn't already know.*

All around the smoking room, patrons of all ages and shapes sat in the high-backed armchairs like they had been poured into them. Outside these walls, these were the cream of the crop, the living embodiment of Mrs Caroline Astor's four hundred. Businessmen and actors, politicians and bankers, lawyers, financiers, landowners…old money and new. Within the Olympus Club however, and away from the prying eagled-eyed paparazzi, they could be true to themselves and embrace their more dark and primitive impulses.

Some drank. Some smoked. Some gambled, either with cards, or the lives of their employees, moving them as they would pawns on a chessboard. And some enjoyed the benefits of their personal attendants.

I only half saw them as I pass by, the clash of white on black amongst the crowd, a tangle of limbs, bodies writhing upon a bulging chair. Hair ruffled and cheeks flushed. The tailored garments they'd ensured were immaculate in front of the cameras, like peacocks presenting their tail-feathers, and that no doubt cost more than anything I could earn in a decade, carelessly dishevelled, with buttons undone, ties loosened, and other articles cast away while the culprit wiggled her fine derrière in his lap.

None of it was full-on sex. Even here, few members would be so brazened out in the open. Regardless, they made no effort to hide their activities as I passed by, the tray raised over my head and the silks of my *uniform* fluttering with every step.

Then again, why should they, I was only a maiden.

As the ancient gods would disguise themselves as men and women to walk among their subjects, to see but be unseen, so the maidens of the Olympus Club would dress as such. Our faces were hidden at all times by a half-mask of our namesakes and our bodies dressed in a uniform of half transparent silks that showed off as much skin as possible, while keeping the necessary parts covered. On the premises, we left our names behind. Here we were servants, the gods of old, who made the world and now live upon it solely to serve.

*I am just a servant of the house. I fetch and serve drinks, but at least the money's good. And there are the fringe benefits…*

Table 12 was called a table only out of courtesy. In fact, it was nothing more than a little square side table to one of the better armchairs. The occupant sat half-cloaked in shadow, eased back and reading a small leather-bound book with one hand. Unlike all the other members, he was dressed smart casual, forgoing his usual contemporary suits for a pair of khaki chinos and a crisp pale blue polo-shirt. The buttons were undone, just hinting at the chiselled muscles beneath in a way that made me long to explore that rugged physique.

Amongst this den of predators and alpha dogs, he was at ease and in his element. The top male, the only one with no need to prove himself.

# Chapter Three

"S-Senator…" My voice trembled around the word. Just being in his presence affected me, put me on edge.

My breath caught in my throat as his eyes darted up to fix on me, scrutinising me.

The look immediately sent a hot shiver through my centre. At the same time, I quelled under his gaze, shrinking until I felt only an inch tall.

*His penitent stare.*

I'd seen that look before, dozens of times in fact.

His instakill. The devastating look he reserved for journalists that asked him ridiculous questions. It always made for damn good television, but I never thought I'd find *that* look directed at me. It was ridiculously hot.

Forcing a dry swallow that rasped my throat all the way down, I presented my tray to him. "Y-your drink, Sir…Scotch on the ro-"

"You're new." It wasn't a question, merely a statement of an obvious fact.

I nearly jumped out of my skin as his low growl thrummed through me. "Yes! I mean…Yes, Sir." I looked away, heat burning my cheeks- and other places further south.

*Jeez, his voice couldn't sound any more made for fuckin' if it came with a side of strawberries and cream for dippin'.*

He had the sexiest voice. Low and gravely but with a flowing command that had been forged on the playing fields of Eton or Oxford. The sort of voice that could inspire fear, demand respect, or reduce a poor, sex-starved girl to a puddle of wanton horniness with just a word. It was the voice in all my fantasies, the one I heard ordering me to cum for him.

Yet here he was silent.

Fighting to control the hot pulsing turning my knees to jelly, I slowly raised my eyes back up. He was still watching me, his eyes a hard icy blue, baleful and intense against the surrounding shadow. He was watching me, raking me from head to toe, studying me the way the wolf studied its prey, judging whether the meal would be worth the effort, before exploding into a run after the bunny.

He held my gaze for a moment, and I felt like he was looking into me, through me. Then he shifted, leaning forward so slowly I felt my breath catch as the shadow was peeled back.

*Oh…My…God…*

It wasn't a kind face. Nothing about Senator Richard Sharpe could ever be called kind. No, it was as hard and jagged as obsidian, a broad chunk of rock that a master mason had chiselled into a work of art. With that square jaw rough with stubble, sharp nose, wicked twist of a mouth, and raven black hair just that bit too long, he looked more like a soldier of fortune than a paper-pushing bureaucrat. And all the sexier for it.

I struggled to keep my nerve as his eyes raked over me with more interest than could ever be considered appropriate in the outside world.

*But here, anything goes.*

"Has anyone claimed you yet?" He asked it as calmly as he would enquire about the weather.

"What, no!" I exclaimed quickly, too quickly. "I mean, no Sir they haven't." Feeling the heat returning to my face, I placed the Senator's whisky on his table. "I'm not-"

"Such a waste." The Senator rose to his feet like a cobra rearing from the grass to loom over me.

*So big...he never looked this impressive on TV.*

Ignoring the drink I'd just laid down for him, he stepped around me, his eyes scorching lines of fire that seemed to burn through my already skimpy uniform as they took me in from head to toe again. Then he did the unthinkable, and gently touched his hand to the base of my back.

"Beautiful."

"Senator...I...I..." I stammered, not sure what to say, barely even able to form words. Fire and electricity crackled at his touch, raising a rush of gooseflesh where our skins touched. Lush heat ignited and pooled in my centre.

No this wasn't right. I couldn't let this go on. I mustn't. Club rules may be lax as far as the members were concerned, but for the staff, and in particular the maidens, they were very strict.

"You take good care of yourself." Another statement. His fingers brushed gently up my spine, then slid just under my ribs as he continued walking around me. My legs quickly turned to jelly under his scrutiny. I knew I needed to put some distance between me and this man, but my body refused to move as he stroked that place just below my left breast.

"I-I try, Sir," I forced out, my throat thick and uncooperative as I tried to restrain the moan that wanted to burst free as he drew closer and closer.

"Please...Senator...I..."

To my surprise, and considerable disappointment, his hand suddenly dropped away and he slid back into his chair with all the panther-like grace with which he had arisen from it, before taking up his drink and holding it out to me. "Here. Drink with me."

"Oh! Err, no Sir, I'm not supposed to-"

"I wasn't asking." He dismissed my refusal by pressing the glass up to my lips. "Drink."

Fingers shaking, I accept the drink, sipping it cautiously. I wasn't much of a drinker, even on nights out I'd only stuck to the fruity, colourful, girly cocktails, and it was all I could do not to gag. The whiskey burned like fire all the way down, the taste strong but smoky and not at all unpleasant.

He watched me as I drank, the way a wolf watched a deer, observing, waiting for that one perfect moment to pounce. The look sent a throb of desire straight through my centre and I couldn't resist a second swallow before he pulled the glass away.

Raising it up to his mouth, he downed the hard alcohol and placed the tumbler back on the table.

This was my chance, I knew it, my chance to get away, but I was captivated by the sight of single drop of amber rolling down his chin and my body wouldn't obey my commands anymore. The sight of him brushing that drop of whiskey away with his thumb, then sucking the pad clean was the sexiest damn thing I've ever seen.

Forcing a dry swallow, I scrambled to regain my composure. "C-c-can I...I mean, will there be anything else, Sir?"

The Senator reached down and fingered the fastenings of his chinos. His eyes flashed like sunlight dancing on blue ice. "Mmm...Yes. There is just one more thing."

# Chapter Four

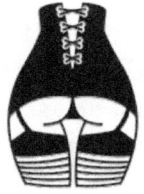

I averted my eyes, the sound of the zip cascading over me like ice water as I looked for something, anything that might otherwise require my attention. "I'll fetch you a girl."

"No."

My mouth felt drier than the desert. "Bu-but what am I-"

"I want you, Kora."

"Please *Senator*." My heart was beating so hard, I could barely speak. "I'm only a maiden. I'm not allowed to-"

"Are you talking back to me? Look at me!" His voice did not raise with the command, but the sudden delicious harshness was as dangerous as it was irresistible. My eyes swivelled obediently, the view that greeted me sending a spike through my centre to my clit. "I said, I want you. You did this to me, so it's only right you should attend to my *little* problem." Except, there was nothing little about his problem.

*I did that?*

There was at least six inches of stiff cock rising out of the fist curled around it's root and midsection, ending in a cut crown that was shiny with pre-cum and flushed a vivid purple.

I'm no virgin. I've seen my share of dicks, and learned to enjoy the bodies attached, but they had been mere boys.

Senator Sharpe was a man, with a man's cock. All ten inches of it!

The sight of it made me forget we were right in the middle of the most exclusive club in New York, surrounded by some of the richest, and most influential people in the world.

Sweeping my tongue across my dry lips, I reached out. Heat radiated off him, and I could practically feel his pulse pounding as I touched a finger to the place just beneath his broad crest. Jesus, he was hard, but also soft, like steel wrapped in warm silk. And hot, so fucking hot.

*A good maiden should always attend to the members' needs…*

"That's it, *Kora*…" That wasn't my name, not my legal name anyway, but the pained ecstasy in his tone, the sheer wanton restraint, had goosebumps rising all across my body and drew my gaze up to his. The heat in his eyes told me all. He wanted me. Wanted all of me, to possess and dominate. And he could take me. He knew I was his, whether I would admit it or not.

Holding his gaze, I bowed my head, his heady flavour spilling over my taste buds as I curled my tongue around that thick crown and took him into my mouth. However, the senator's only response was to arch his brow, that granite jaw locked in a silent challenge.

I gladly accepted. Heart pounding, I mouthed the plush head, sucking and drinking up the heady salty goodness of his pre-cum.

Still, he gave no outward sign, but I could feel the tension amassing within him, the pressure building as his cock grew thicker, harder within my mouth, so I decided to kick things up a notch. I sank to my knees between his. Placing both my hands on his trouser clad thighs, the muscles beneath bunching at my touch, I pivoted so he could see himself bulging against the inside of my cheek and dragged my mouth down the right side of his shaft, down to where his hand still grasped it, offering himself to me. I teased my tongue around the whitening knuckles, then came slowly back up his left flank before taking him into my mouth.

There was movement on the very edge of my vision, and it gave me a perverse thrill to know that the people around were starting to take notice. I glimpsed them nudging and gesturing, shifting to get a better view. They were attempting to be subtle about it but made little real effort to hide their interest.

I was beyond caring. I have always loved giving head. Loved the thrill of having so much power over people so much stronger than me and making them come undone. It was a potent mix, intoxicating. Swept along by the heat of the moment and drawn in the eroticism that the senator seemed to radiate, my only thought was on the task. I didn't care who saw, who watched. I wanted to beat this man, this titan. I wanted to shatter his control, break his willpower, and make him cum in my mouth.

I'd wanted to take him all in, but there was just too much of him. He was too big to deep throat- just the head seemed to fill my mouth to the brim- so I teased between going fast and slow, sucking him in as deep as I dared before pulling back.

"Oh *fuck*..." His, low, almost edgy groan was music to my ears and my neglected pussy pulsed and burned in wanton need as his fingers threaded through my hair, fisting and forcing me back down.

He held me there, his hips churning up, fucking my mouth with the savage intensity I had only ever fantasised about. Hot salty tears burned my eyes. I couldn't breathe, he was going too deep, had me forced down so far my nose was nestled in the nest of dark curls, but I couldn't have cared less.

Then I felt the rush of victory as with a ragged groan and a penetrating thrust that took him all the way into my throat, he came.

He came hard.

Unable to pull away with the Senator's white knuckled grip forcing me down, I sucked him greedily, drinking every hot creamy shot. I kept on sucking even after he had spilled everything he had to give, milking him for all he was worth.

"Mmm…" He purred, the hand falling from my hair to collar my throat. He forced me to abandon my new toy and pulled me up to look him in the eye. "That was very good." He was still hard but tucked himself back inside his chinos, his eyes dark and burning into mine with barely restrained lust. "But now it's time, Kora."

# Chapter Five

The senator didn't offer any explanations as he led me, and I didn't ask.

Shame and embarrassment burned my cheeks. I could feel every eye in the lounge on me as we passed, but I didn't dare meet them. Not even when I glimpsed Demeter glowering at me, her eyes scorching trails across my back, down to where the large hand was moulding my buttocks. I was so getting fired for this.

Then he took me through the back door, into a small square foyer that housed a single elevator, the entrance to the underworld. It was a dark, unfurnished place with naked stone walls. Four life size sculptures etched from polished black marble stood sentry in each corner. They were impressive figures, taken straight out of the pages of Frank Miller's *300* and poised with swords raised and hoplites bared. Behind their helms, garnets had been set in the place of eyes and blazed in defiance. At the base of each, a plaque had been set upon a plinth, stamped with one of four legends in gold print – Penthos, Curae, Nosoi and Geras.

The elevator door slid open as we approached, the bright interior throwing long shadows across the floor. I blinked, the light blinding. The Senator held me close and guided me through. Yet the closeness was almost as disabling as the brightness. Awareness shivered up my skin and just the sound of his breathing had me coming out in goosebumps.

If the foyer was small, then the elevator was practically claustrophobic. A tiny space barely large enough for one with walls lined by plush red velvet. The only distinguishing feature was a brass control plate etched with the name *Charon* etched across the top and a row of buttons to reach the five floors above.

Under these was a scanner plate.

This was my first time going into the Underworld. It was the private area of the Olympus Club that only members and their personal attendants were permitted to enter. Unlike its name sake which had been believed to be on the edge and beneath the world of ancient Greece, Olympus's Underworld took up the floors directly above the club.

Senator Sharp removed a gold coin from his pocket and pressed it to the scanner.

"Where are you taking me?" I asked when the car began to rise, my heart pounding in my breast.

"Somewhere private. I have a proposition for you, Kora." He didn't look at me, but I could feel him watching me all the same. It made me feel hot, made my sex slick and tits heavy.

"Yes? What's that? Sir." I licked my lips, my mouth dry.

"Patience" He dismissed, the hand on my back starting to brush up and down the curve of my spine through my silks. "*All good things to those who wait.*"

Up and down, up and down, getting lower and lower until his hand brushed under the folds of my uniform. I felt my legs start to tremble. Tingles shivered out from where skin touched skin, spiralling straight up to my poor, neglected clit.

I clamp my legs together, trapping his hand between them even as I rubbed my thighs together, desperate for some friction to quell the need raging down there.

"Open"

I had never enjoyed being bossed around, but the quiet authority in his tone made it feel so right, even as my body screamed in protest. I obeyed, splaying my thighs as far as they would comfortably go. Then his fingers took over, his hand cupping my greedy sex.

"Already so wet?" His tongue slid around the shell of my ear as one of his digits slid through my creamy folds to circle my clit. "Want more?"

"Please…" My tone was breathy, desperate and pleading. I couldn't stop myself from fisting his top and clinging to him for dear life as my legs almost gave way, the spike of pleasure from the contact going from my core to my fingertips.

"Please?" The senator asked, pressing down on my little bundle of nerves before drawing the finger back.

I bit back my protest, along with half a dozen sarcastic retorts. "Please…Sir-ohh!" As he pushed his thick finger into me, my mouth fell open in a low moan and his mouth crushed against mine.

It was not a soft kiss. It was hungry and violent. His mouth claimed mine, the silky softness of his tongue mirroring the strokes of his finger, delving inside me with an expertise that had my whole core tightening. It was too much. I couldn't stand it. Despite myself, my hips started to roll, my blood pumping fast and hot as the world started to spin around us and –

He pulled away as the elevator chimed, his finger slipping out of my heat and leaving me feeling woefully empty. Breathing hard, I leaned up on my tiptoes to follow, but the Senator just stepped around me, through the opening doors into…

*Oh my god! It's Hades's Palace…*

I'd thought it was just a joke. A gag to play on the F.N.G.s, (The *Fucking New Gods)*, but there it was.

The word was, it was a premium extra exclusive add on, that was available to only one member of the Olympus Club. None of the staff; maidens or even the attendants, knew which member it was, so most of them thought it was a myth, like most of the other stories they'd heard about The Underworld.

I couldn't believe it. Hades Palace, the secret, exclusive penthouse/ fuck pad was real!

Stepping out of the elevator, I seemed to move from the light into the Nightscape of New York City. Though no lights were on inside, the radiance of the city, and the full moon above glowed through the high windows and Balcony's French doors, giving it an almost starlit twilight.

It was too dark for me to make out much furniture, but I could tell what there was, was carved from polished black stone, as were the floor tiles and architecture. Everything was stone, except for the four-poster bed. A king-size of course, fitted with raven silk sheets and piled high with what could only have been the biggest, softest pillows I have ever seen.

I wasn't sure where to look, so instead I focused on the one familiar fixture of the room.

Senator Sharpe stood staring out across the city with his arms behind his back, like an emperor looking out across his domain. Or a god.

I approached him cautiously, suddenly so very aware of how large he was as his impressive build was framed alongside the spear of the empire state building.

"Do you ever take the time to just look at it?" he asked, still not looking at me.

"Umm…No"

"You should. It is a beautiful city by moonlight," he sighed. "I love this view. It almost makes the mercenary rates the management charge for this little place worth it."

"Well, I never have time to just stop and look."

"Shame."

"I have commitments, loans- student loans!" I quickly clarify, for some reason overcome by a need to explain, to make him understand. "And my mother's medical treatments-"

"I know. Second stage lung and throat cancer. Two different strains of cancer forming simultaneously is a very unfortunate coincidence." He pivoted to face me, and I felt my breath catch at the raw intensity in his eyes. "And costly."

I didn't say anything. I didn't even ask how he knew about my mom. Given the secretive nature of the Olympus Club, my contract included not just numerous nondisclosure agreements, but a legal agreement, stating my consent to an unspecified number of background checks a year. Of course, the details of such checks were supposed to be confidential, but it wasn't hard for me to imagine some of the more influential members being given brief peeks.

"What would you say if I told you your mother could be receiving a consultation from the best oncologist in the country? All expenses and treatment fully covered and free of charge."

"I'd tell you to stay on your meds. Goodnight." I wheel away, tears starting to burn in the corner of my eyes as the world started to spin. How dare he, no one uses my mother like that, no one!

"I can make it happen." He says after me. "This time tomorrow, she can be on a private jet. A consultation with Dr Leo Getts scheduled for first thing the day after tomorrow."

I didn't look back, not until I was in front of the elevator, my finger poised over the call button.

I wanted to, but I just couldn't bring myself to push.

He was shitting me. He had to be. It was just too good to be true. That sort of treatment, hell, just an hour's consultation would cost an arm and a leg, never mind the expense of crossing the country, and lodging, private nursing staff...Why would be willing to go through all that?

But what if he was on the level?

A single tear slid down my check as I turned back to face the senator, only to find him towering over me. I hadn't even heard him coming after me.

I bite back my surprised gasp. "Wh-what would I have to do?"

"Be my attendant." His arms cage me as he flattens both hands on the elevator, bracing himself as he bends forward, closing the gap so we were nose to nose, his eyes dark and hot.

"You're joking?"

He had to be. While attendants continued to receive the basic salary, the additional costs of their exclusivity and *services* were covered by their *'Masters'*. The price, and terms, were negotiated between the two parties, and could sometimes even go so far as positions in real world jobs. But what he was offering went beyond generous.

"Never."

He more growled than said the word, and our closeness was so intoxicating I could practically feel it vibrating through me. "You're the only maiden I can trust. *They* haven't had their claws in you yet, and they never will, if I claim you tonight. I need you, *Kora*."

His proximity and the raw intensity in his tone made it impossible for me to look him in the eye. "But you can't...I mean, maidens need a minimum of two years' service before they can be considered for a attendant. I've only been here a month..."

I was shaking, need and desperation had my blood running hot and thick through my veins.

He chuckled. "Yes, I know. Recommended by the Honourable Justice Lovejoy, the father of a university friend who you dormed with for a few months until you moved in with a local boyfriend. You remained friends with her but broke up with him after you found him in bed with his boyfriend."

The remark grounded me slightly, giving me a much-needed surge of anger that helped get a momentary grip of myself and wheel away from him to face the comforting cool steel front of the elevator. "You've done your homework. Do *they* have my bra size in their background checks too?"

"Anything's obtainable, Kora, even you." He whispered in my ear, before curving over me to sweep his tongue around the shell, his hands enfolding my waist. "And you never wear a bra."

Wound up tight in a knot of tension, I practically jumped out of my skin when, as if to prove his point, he cupped my right breast through my robe.

I won't lie, I've always had very nice tits, well rounded and perhaps a bit more generously proportioned than most woman with my build, but with absolutely no sag, and topped by dusky nipples that my lovers seemed to just love sucking.

For all my bountiful offering however, his hand completely covered my cleavage and I couldn't help my whimper when he plumped my breast.

"W-what if I refuse?" Almost beyond speech, I was panting with the words. *Touching…He's touching my…he shouldn't…I must – oh God…*

"You won't." He purred, rolling one of my tender nipples between his thumb and finger, their roughness exciting my skin through my robe.

"N-n-noo-oh!"

His musky scent was everywhere, all around me, fogging my brain and invading my thoughts. Damn, he smelt so good.

"No, you want what I'm offering." He took my left hand in his and guided it down to the crotch of his trousers. My core tightened and throbbed at the feeling of his renewed hard-on straining against the fabric. "It's all yours for the taking. All you have to do is say *yes*…"

Then he spun me around to face him and took my mouth before I could form a word.

It was all aggression and heat. Not so much a kiss as a claiming. I whimpered as his tongue found mine, stroking me with lush coaxing licks that had me melting against him as my damn needy pussy purred with delight. In the next instant, his arms were around me, his hands curling around my waist, grabbing my butt and crushing me against the wall of hard virile male, making me feel how *hard* he was.

I needed to be strong. I knew it. This was my chance, I had to stop, had to pull away or slap him or knee him, or, or just, something…

Anything…

Anything but grab his hair and return the kiss, my spine curling up so he could feel my cleavage push against him, one leg sliding up his, coiling round his-

Oh God. No, no! I had to push him away. Push him away now before it was too late.

But I couldn't. It was all too much for me. He was too much for me.

My pussy was hot, my breasts heavy and tender with nipples that just ached to for attention, and all I could think about was that this was Senator Richard Sharp. The Senator Richard Sharp. The man I had been crushing on since I saw his first ever televised political debate, and he was kissing me.

No, he wasn't kissing me. His mouth was basically fucking mine, and I loved it.

Somewhere in a distant, still coherent corner of my mind, I could feel him guiding me backward. I didn't resist. Rather, I practically climbed up him, my legs coiling around his waist, hips gyrating against the bulge of his dick as he took me deeper into the room, until he had me pinned against one of the his massive fourposter's beams.

My whole body shivered deliciously at the feeling of being cornered by this big alpha male, overwhelmed by the feeling of his massive cock sliding along my slit through our mesh of clothes. It was the most divine torture. The barrier teased me by preventing any real depth, while the mix of textures rubbing over my tender tissues drove me wild. God, he felt so good. So big. So-it wasn't enough.

I needed more of him.

"Mmm… say it, Kora." The senator growled, pulling back just enough to break the kiss, before he buried his face in the crock of my neck.

"I shouldn't." He sucked hard on my pulse spot, making me gasp as desire shot through me. "I mustn't…please!"

"Please what?" he growled again, setting me down on legs that shook like jelly as he nipped trails of fire.

I whimpered, shaking my head, my body hot and thrumming like a taught violin string.

*Oh God…Oh God! This can't be happening. This can't be-*

"Say it!" His hands encircled my wrists, raising them up above my head before pressing them to the timber post.

"Yes!" I couldn't stop the flood. His words, the way he held me, pinned me to his bed and devoured my very being. It was too much. "Yes. I want more. You can have me however you want, I'm all yours. Just give me more."

# Chapter Six

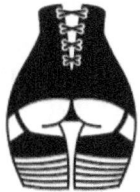

"Good girl," he praised, and gave my ear lobe a long suck, before drawing back. "Now, don't move."

The command sent a shiver through me, its gruff, no-nonsense tone echoing the voice from my fantasises. I obeyed.

His face impassive, the Senator collared both of my wrists in one of his hands, before reaching for something out of my line of sight. Heat rushed through me when he raised what it was up for me to see.

Dangling, between his thumb and forefinger, was a red silk scarf.

*Oh God, where did that come from?*

"Don't move,' he repeated, and the thrill it gave me to hear that lush commanding tone had me biting my lip in anticipation.

It wasn't just a command. This was a test. He was daring me, baiting me to test the boundaries of this new role.

I was his attendant now. I must obey his every command immediately and without hesitation, or I'll be punished.

*And in return, he'll take care of all of mom's medical bills.*

He swept the scarf around my wrists once, tied off, then repeated the tie around the bed post. It wasn't anything as secure as handcuffs, but the silk was much kinder to my skin and a testing tug from the senator proved I wouldn't be getting away any time soon.

He took a moment to admire his handiwork.

"Mmm…Very good, Kora," he purred. Awareness rippled up my spine and I felt my skin rise with goosebumps as he trailed a finger down the underside of my right arm. "You're mine now. You're going to have to do everything I say."

I nodded, my heart racing as his finger trailed down my silks to the swell of my breasts, my nipples standing unashamedly against the fabric.

"I do mean *everything*, Kora."

"Yes Master-oh!" I couldn't help my kittenish gasp when he cupped the swell of my left breast and thumbed the tip. "Mmm…Give it to me, please…do anything you want to me, I'm yours."

"Yes, you are." he breathed, squeezing my cleavage through my garment, the warmth of his touch bleeding through the silk to lick my skin. "But you have to earn your place as my attendant."

"Yes, make me earn it." It was the sweetest torture. My body hummed with tension and the need to move, to arch and offer myself to him, to force his hand to where I needed it, was almost overwhelming. Damnit, I had to resist.

*Don't move. Just don't move, you can do this, you can…*

"You'll beg for it." His eyes flashed at the promise.

Despite my resolve to obey, when his thumb and finger closed around my nipple and twisted it, it was all too much.

"Yes!" My head rolled, the moan flowing from me in painful ecstasy as my spine curled.

Even his softest touch sent fire and electricity through my core.

"Kora." His tone was clipped, disapproving. "I told you, don't move. I see I'm going to have to teach you obedience."

"I-I'm sorry Master. It won't happen again."

"I know." The Senator gave my nipple another twist, this time a little harder. Not enough to hurt, but enough for me to know. Then his hand was moving again, fingers brushing over the swells of my bosom, beneath the folds of silk to the bounty of naked skin, and down. Down the valley of my breasts. Down the flat-plain of my belly. And down to the string of well-sodden fabric that was all that covered my throbbing sex.

"I've been a bad girl. Very, very bad, teach me to be good. I'll do any...anythi- oh God!"

He cupped my pussy through my panties, his middle finger sliding through the outline of my swollen folds to press down on my clit. I was so sensitive, that that little contact set off supernovas behind my eyes.

I couldn't take it. I had to touch him. I needed to grab him, feel the muscles rippling under his skin and lust pounding in his chest. I couldn't bare it, except the scarf held me fast and wouldn't loosen, no matter how much I twisted and tugged against it. All I could do was claw desperately at the timber as he traced the line of my sex through my panties with a maddening softness that made my skin tingle and feel too tight.

"You're soaked. What am I going to do with you Kora? You must really be gagging for it.".

"Yes, I – I need it Master. Give it to me, I want it, I want it." My hips rocked into his touch, desperate to steer his attentions back towards my little bundle of nerves. Fuck, I didn't care if I sounded like a wanton slut. I didn't care at all.

He took me and made me forget my inhibitions.

With a look, he'd made me forget all my determination not to fall into such a role. A word from him had reduced me into a steaming mess of sexual frustration. And just a touch had me on the verge of losing my mind. Fuck, I was so close, just a little more, that's all I needed. Just a little more and I would cum all over his fingers.

"Good girl, you're being much more honest now. But still so disobedient," he chuckled, lowering his head until we were almost nose to nose. "It wouldn't be a punishment if I just gave you what you wanted now, would it?" Hooking his finger under my underwear, he quickly pulled it aside.

I moaned, shaking my head even as I strained to reach him, offering my lips to him in open invitation. "N-no…"

It's hard to say whether I was agreeing with him or protesting.

Either way, I watched wide-eyed as the senator made a show of bringing his wet and shiny finger up to his lips and sucked it clean. "Mmm…you're delicious."

I lost all control at that. My core clamped down in wanton spasms while my hips bucked and my body started to tremble. I was so tight with sexual tension, one good pluck would have me twanging like a guitar string "Oh God, you're such a tease."

"Yes, and you love it."

"I love it." I could practically feel his lips brushing over mine, so close, just one more inch.

His hand cupped the nape of my neck, then his mouth was back on mine, swallowing my moan as his finger pushed inside me.

He started slow, with just that one *thick* finger hooked forward to stroke the place behind my clit, the broad pad deliciously rough against my delicate tissues. It stirred me into a frenzy as he pushed the digit back and forth, somehow managing to keep perfect rhythm with his tongue so the dual stimulation worked to maximum effect.

Whoever said men couldn't multitask had obviously never been finger banged by Senator Richard Sharpe.

"Remember. Don't. Move," he growled against my mouth in that hot authoritative tone, emphasising each word as a second finger pushed into me and sent me spiralling.

"I-I can't! I – I- oh fuck- I'm cumming!" I couldn't resist it. My orgasm washed over me like a wave on the rocks and had me arching in his arms, straining against my bonds in violent bucking tremors of ecstasy.

"Oh? You bad girl," he chided, dragging kisses along my jaw and down my neck. "You know you're going to have to be punished for this?"

I couldn't think. My world was shattering as I rode his fingers, the waves rushing over me, growing more powerful. Then his thumb pressed into my clit and I went wild. "Oh fuck! Yes! I'm such a bad girl…mmm…punish me…Master!"

"Oh…I will, later, but for now…" The hand on my neck moved down to the base of my spine, half supporting me and half pulling me against him as he bent down, his lips catching my right nipple and sucking.

His thumb rolled over my clit while he pushed his fingers in and out, in and out, working me into a frenzy. Helpless to resist, all I could do was writhe, throwing my head from side to side, clawing the post as heat and ecstasy radiated through from my core, out to my fingers and toes.

He pulled his mouth away, his eyes dark and burning up at me as he tongued my nipple through my silks and bore down on my clit with his thumb. "You just keep cumming, and so easily, you really have been gagging for it, haven't you, Kora?"

I was melting in his arms, the very fibre of my being turning to liquid and running down my thighs as my hips pumped greedily onto his fingers and thumb, sensation amassing in my core. "It's not…not my fau-oh fuck! I can't help it, you just…"

He licked his way back up my neck, his breathing quick and hungry with lust. "What do I do to you? Go on, say it Kora."

"You just keep making me cum!"

"Mmm...Good girl, now look into my eyes..."

I obeyed.

I would always obey. No matter what he wanted, I was his. He could have anything. For him, I would do anything.

"Cum for me Kora, cum all over my fingers!" His words were hot against my lips and the intensity in his kiss as he took my lips made my mind go blank.

"Please...no more...I can't take it anymore..." I panted when my brain started working again, and the blood stopped roaring in my ears.

He'd made me cum so hard, every muscle in my body felt like jelly and I didn't have the strength to stand. If it wasn't for his arm around me, I think I might very well have collapsed.

"Oh, my dear, sweet, innocent little Kora, I'll never stop." The dark promise in his tone sent renewed shivers through me, but then his fingers slipped from my heat and I was left feeling empty, and somehow even hornier as he brought the fingers to his mouth and licked them clean. "God, you just keep cumming but you're still so tight, this is going to be better than I thought."

Somewhere very, very deep down and far away, a mousy voice in my head asked what he meant, but I was too far gone to care.

He lowered me to the floor, so I sat propped again the bed, the silk tie sliding down the polished beam with me. When he straightened, I found myself staring at his covered cock. Somehow, even confined by his chinos, it looked larger than before, and was clearly visible as a massive bulge straining against the length of his right thigh.

I licked my lips hungrily and leaning forward, mouthed him through his trouser leg. When I traced the curve of his crown with my tongue, he made a strangled sound in the back of his throat. "That's it. Such a dirty girl…"

I nodded, much too eagerly. "Yes, I'm a dirty girl, Master. Your attendant. Let me serve you. I need it…I can't wait any longer…"

"But you will," he ordered, his lips pressed firmly together as he looked down at me, like a teacher preparing to punish a disobedient student. "You're mine now Kora, my attendant, my little toy."

I swallowed, the very thought of it making me bite my lower lip in anticipation. "And I have to do everything you say."

"Yes."

The chinos were undone with a quick movement of his hands and his renewed erection surged upward to stand tall before my eyes, it's length thickly veined, the head slick and flushed with colour. With one hand, he angled his dick down to point at my mouth. "So, attend to me."

I didn't need to be told twice.

I sucked him in greedily, taking him in as deep as I could, moaning as his salty goodness spilled over my tongue. His cock felt even more amazing in my mouth the second time around, and the way he watched me going down on him, with those eyes dark with lust, only made it that much hotter. I returned the gaze hotly as I pulled back to his crest then pushed forward again, watching with rapt attention as he pulled his top over his head to reveal a glorious bounty of male perfection.

I drank him in and wanted nothing more than to reach out and run my nails down that broad chest of defined muscle, his light dusting of course black hair seeming only to add to his appeal. Strange, I'd never really found chest hair to be attractive, but on him it only added to his allure. It made him look wild and untamed, and contrasted so vividly with the image of control he portrayed on the pages of GQ.

He was everything I'd ever imagined and so much more.

Spurred on by his little strip tease, I sucked harder, my cheeks hollowing as I drew him in. There was no fancy tricks this time. I just went all out and worshiped his dick with my mouth.

Then his hand slid though my hair, fisting and twisting, holding me still as his hips started rolling.

"Yeah...let your master fuck your mouth," the Senator groaned in a guttural rasp that sent a shiver straight down to the still heat between my legs. "Get me nice and wet for your tight little cunt."

His hips churned, the circles growing larger, forcing me to take him deep, deeper than I'd ever taken a man before.

This was new territory for me. Whenever I'd given head before, I'd always been the one in charge. It was all part of the thrill, but the senator somehow took that control away. Now he had the power and I gave in to his commands like a good attendant.

And I loved it.

He fucked my mouth hard, but with perfect control, his pace unwavering. I could feel him passing through the gate of my throat, the crown pulsing and swelling, and it made me crazy with need, desperate to feel him between my legs, filling me up-

He pulled back, withdrawing completely from my mouth. Then his arms were around me and he'd pulled me back to my feet, into a deep lush kiss that had me melting all over again. This was the first time anyone had ever kissed me straight after I'd sucked them, and the idea that he must be able to taste himself, was so kinky, I almost came.

And while his mouth took mine, his hands brushed up my arms to where I was manacled to the bedpost. Much to my embarrassment, the tie came undone with a quick tug.

However, I had no time to enjoy my freedom, as no sooner had the silk come away than he was spinning me around, pushing me up against the post.

I clung to it gratefully, my legs still a bit too shaky. Smooth and polished to a high shine, the timber felt deliciously cool against my overheated skin. "M-Master, please!"

"Patience, Kora. You really need to learn patience, if you want to be my attendant." His low promise had me tingling all over, as did the way his hands slid down my back and under my silks to the string of my panties.

The delicate fabric snapped like dental floss under his huge hands. Then he hiked my silks up and over my butt and nudged my legs open further with his knees.

I obeyed and leant forward more, raising my ass in the air. I should have been embarrassed, knowing he could see *me*, all of me, my most private and personal places, but I wanted him to see.

"Ahh!" I gasped as he gave my backside a swat.

It hurt, a little, but then the sting dissolved into hot pleasure and I couldn't resist giving a quick inviting wiggle. Fuck, what was wrong with me. I'd never been into spanking before. Hell, I was acting like a complete slut, and I didn't care. The Senator was everything my dreams and fantasies had promised, and I just knew he was going to be so much more before he was finished with me.

"Like that Kora?" the Senator asked, slowly rubbing the hot spot his hand had left across my right cheek, massaging the heat into my skin. "Want more?"

Somewhere, there was the soft sound of a draw opening and closing. Then a packet tearing. But I was too consumed by the wantonness rippling through me to give it much thought. It just felt so good, I just couldn't stand it. "Yes!"

He withdrew his hand, letting the warmth bleed away. "Yes?"

I could feel him. Feel it. Feel its heat licking up my folds before its blunt tip pressed into my little bundle of nerves and fireworks sparked behind my eyes. I edged back, raising my hips to try and slide onto him, only for him pull back.

For a long moment, there was nothing. It was as if time held its breath for us and the sudden solitude of the moment made my heart thunder in my ears. And I was too scared to move, too breathe, in case all this shattered around me and revealed itself as nothing but just another incredible dream.

Then his mouth was by my ear, his voice a rumble that had my pussy clenching.

"Yes what?"

"Master!" I wailed, pleading. He'd driven me mad and I was just too horny to care. In all my life, nothing had ever gotten me this worked up. I needed him inside me, to feel his hardness filling me up. "Please Master…my cunt's so wet for you…give it to me…please, give it to me-oh oh God, oh fuck-"

There was pleasure, a sudden rush of sensation that spiralled out to my fingers and toes, but there was also pain. First there was a potent and very fiery bite, then a deep satisfying burn that made me ache for more as he slid into me, the wide crest parting my folds, stretching my delicate tissues and spreading me open, then pushing inexorably into my heat.

"Look at me, Kora."

I threw a desperate look back at him, my mouth dropping open in a long voiceless cry as he filled me, that first thrust splitting me open and driving into my core. Fuck, I could barely breath through the feeling. None of my previous lovers had prepared me for this. He was just too much.

"Mmm…you pull that sexy face when you're getting fucked and your pussy's so snug," he purred, grinning down at me as he continued pressing forward, with just the perfect amount of force, until he seemed to have gone as deep as he could go. "Just like fucking a virgin."

Heat flushed through my body, and I wanted to beg him not to say such dirty things, but I couldn't get the words out. Then one of his hands was cupping my nape and urged me down until I was bent at the waist, opening me up as he withdrew.

He drew back slowly, leaving me with a growing feeling of emptiness as he pulled out, until just the head remained inside me. Then he pressed in again, his hips snapping forward, and my head rolled back in agonising bliss.

"So-so big…I can't…too-too much…" I panted, my nails scouring the timber of the frame. This new angle had him stimulating a whole load of new nerves I had never felt before and he was so deep inside me, I could feel him throbbing through the rubber.

"You can, Kora. And you will," he promised, his dark and cultured voice growing ragged with passion. He repeated the move again, sliding out then thrusting back into me, then again, and again, building to a rhythm as his other hand on my hip began pulling me back to meet him.

Each time he went a little deeper. Working inch after inch inside me, until I felt like I was going to burst and was on the verge of going out of my mind.

My body however only craved more and pressed back to meet him, my greedy sex convulsing and throbbing, wrapping around him and sucking him in. "M-Master!"

The Senator chuckled at my plea, the sound so very gruff and primal, his hips slapping wetly against my butt as he made me take him even deeper. "Mmm…you feel so good, Kora, your pussy was made for my dick," he declared, like a captain claiming a newly discovered land.

"Y-y-yes that's your pussy…oh my god, yes! My little pussy is all yours Master. Oh fuck, it's yours…use me…make me take my master's cock…make me take it…take it…take it-oh!"

The mini orgasm swept through me hard and fast when he finally made me take him all and his wide crest struck *that* place deep inside me. He didn't let me rest or come down from the high, but fucked me through my release, circling his hips in tight little rolls as my walls clamped down around him and refused to let go.

I absorbed everything he had to give me, savouring every thick and gloriously hard inch of him, and craved more. Then his arms were around me, cradling me, drawing me back against him and driving me down onto his cock.

He was in complete control, my master in name and body, and I'd never dreamed someone, anyone, could dominate me so completely. I let him take me, my hands falling to my sides, fisting and balling against the pleasure while my head rolled back onto his shoulder as each curl of his hips drove me up onto my tiptoes.

"Oh God…oh God, you-you're going to make me cum again…"

I could feel *it* building, a hot throbbing knot in my centre and I pushed down, grinding against his cock, suddenly just needing to reach that peak. "Master, I'm gonna cum all over your dick…please…plea-!"

"You're gorgeous, Kora," he husked in my ear, his hands moving over me, touching and feeling, fanning the flames of my desire. Gathering up my silks, he dragged the garment from me and cast it aside before one of his hands came up to cup my left breast, plumping it while his thumb teased over my hard nipple. "Now…touch yourself."

"Master?" I gasped, breathless and close, so close that my legs were shaking with it. I was on the edge. I just needed a little more.

"I want you to make yourself cum, Kora."

"Master, please, I don't...I can't...it's embarrassing..." I pleaded, shaking my head even as his free hand took mine, and put it over the throbbing heat at my centre.

"Cum," he ordered, and I couldn't resist. There was something so illicit and sexy about the feeling of being skin to skin with the senator. It made me feel wild and desperate and I rubbed my clit, fast and hard, three fingers thrumming over the little bud as he continued driving in me from behind.

"That's it, cum for me Kora, cum for your master."

The dual cocktail of pleasures ignited a firework in my brain, and I stilled as the pleasure-shock of it washed over me, shaking me to my core in a delicious whiteout of sensation. And when I came down from the heights, I found myself stretched out across the bed with Senator Richard standing over me.

Breathing hard, my whole being a mass of tingling aftershocks, I could only watch in awe as he loomed over me. He looked so huge and great, so much more than flesh and bone. Like a god.

He was my Hades.

I'd played the role of a goddess, bound and chained for the service of mortals. He'd freed me. He'd freed me, unchained me and taken me to the underworld, his dark realm where he'd brought out all my forbidden and secret desires. Now I was his.

His attendant. His servant.

His Kora.

He didn't say a word. Just pushed his trousers down his long legs. I didn't know when he'd removed his shoes and socks, and I didn't care. I just knew what he wanted and obediently opened myself to him, my eyes riveted to his cruelly handsome face as he came for me, crawling up the bed until he was between my legs

"Mmm...such a sweet little cunt," he purred, bowing his head down to inhale the scent of my sex. "I've wanted to eat this pussy since I first set eyes on you Kora."

The feeling of his breath wafting over my sex sent a hot shiver of desire straight through me. "Master, I-"

He dragged his tongue up my folds, making my hips jump and I moaned a long sweet sound, before his mouth descended on my swollen and tender clit. He sucked with an intensity that had me clawing at the sheets, my body instinctively twisting away, desperate to escape the too-fierce pleasure of his mouth.

"Stay still," he growled, the low thrum of his words vibrating through the place our bodies joined and straight to my core.

"Oh, God!" My head rolled as his hands wound around my legs, cupped my ass and pulled me against his mouth. "Master...please...put your dick back in...I need it...plea-oh! Oh my god!"

He thrust his tongue inside me, deep inside me, and lashed my inner walls with twirling swirls that quickly sent me spiralling.

I was going to cum again.

I couldn't stop it, the multiple orgasms he'd already lavished upon me had left me raw and sensitive, too sensitive. And the image of his eyes, dark and smouldering, watching me from between my legs was just too much. I couldn't stand it. I couldn't-

I couldn't fucking believe it.

I wanted to scream and beat the bed as he reared back, leaving me hanging on the edge. "N-no! Don't...stop..."

Instead, he caged me with his body, that sinful mouth pressing to mine as the full weight of his desire settled against me. He kissed me for a long moment, his wily tongue resuming its sinful dance, working me into a breathless frenzy before he pulled back just enough to drink in the sight of me stretched out beneath him.

What a sight I must have looked.

When he touched my mask, I didn't resist. Nor did I try and stop him when he pulled it from me, but nor could I meet his eyes. I'd seen the pictures on social media and google. I knew the sort of woman Senator Richard Sharp liked. I didn't match up.

He liked blonde super models with delicate features and plenty of ass. Not raven-haired, doe eyed bookworms that made Hermione Granger look like Lara Croft.

I was realistic, I knew the score, but even so, I couldn't bare to see his look of disappointment.

"Look at me, Kora." Cupping my chin, he angled my head to look up at him. My mouth was dry by the time I met his eyes, their depths almost black with lust. There was no disappointment there. No rejection. Just want. "You're so beautiful, don't ever let anyone tell you different."

Still looking deep into my eyes, he thrust forward.

I gasped a voiceless cry, my back arching at the feeling of him surging inside me, filling me and pushing me back into the sudden rush of a mini-orgasm. It swept through me hard and fast and I was still shaking as he began rolling his hips, pulling back then thrusting home. It wasn't fast, but nor was it slow. It was firm, and steady, and pushed the sensations coursing through me on and on.

I was enslaved by the vision of him above me, his arms braced on either side of me, his muscles moving beneath his skin, bunching and tensing and powering the relentless draw and thrust of his hips. I watched him in awe, unable to tear my eyes from the sight of his dick sliding in and out of my sex, the condom stretched tight and shiny with my creamy desire.

He was a work of art. A machine built with the sole function of fucking me into oblivion.

"Mmm…no one's ever fucked you like I do, have they Kora?"

"No…not like you…no one…oh my god…" My hips churned as I tried to match him, my feet slipping and sliding on the silken sheets as I fucked him back, until he seized both my legs and raised them up onto his shoulders, opening me up completely I could feel him reaching my stomach. "Oh my god…feels so good…so fucking good and deep…I'm all yours Master, your little slut…I'm your good, little, slutty attendant!"

"Yes, you are Kora. Mine. All mine." He reinforced his ownership with each deep thrust, the delicious friction of it igniting a fire in my head that was melting my mind.

"I just want to be yours. Your good little toy…use my body to make your dick cum…I'm just here to please you…take me however you want…I'm yours-oh fuck-I'm all yours!"

And I was. I was his toy, ready and willing to do whatever he wanted, whenever he wanted me.

"Oh fuck-oh fuck- Master," Orgasm after orgasm began pouring through me, coming on so fast and hard, I could barely tell where one ended and the next began. "It's too-too much…I can't, can't stop cumming!"

"Yeah! That's it, Kora," the senator groaned, his head dipping down to nip and suck at my tingling nipples. "Keep cumming for me baby, milk my dick with your greedy little cunt."

The Senator was getting close too. I could feel it in the way his once measured thrusts began to quicken, as if he was racing to get me off just one more time.

So I bared down on him, fighting the terminus of my ceaseless orgasms to wrap my inner walls around him, wanting nothing so much as I did at that moment to make him blow. I wanted to see the pleasure twist him. I wanted to feel all his passion and desire flow through me. I wanted to know that I'd done that to him, reduced the most powerful man in New York City to a sweaty sated mess. I wanted-

"Oh fuck, here I come!" he rasped, gritting his teeth, momentarily trying to fight the stirring in his balls as he pulled out of me. Without my Master inside me, I felt cold and empty, but then he was on top of me and I forgot all of that. The Senator tore the condom off before fisting himself as he angled the red throbbing crown to me. "Open."

I did as I was ordered. And like the Persephone of ancient times, who ate the apple seeds offered by Hades and was so bound to the underworld for all eternity, I leaned up, took him in and drank down everything he had to give me.

He came hard, the hot salty build up filling up my mouth and running down my chin as I sucked him through it, his low rasping grunts and moans music to my ears. When he'd shot his third and final load, I licked him clean, swirling my tongue around his throbbing crest then up and down his shaft. I didn't miss a drop, like the good little attendant I was.

Only when I was certain he was clean did I pull off and promptly collapsed back into the warm embrace of the wonderfully cool silk sheets.

I couldn't remember the last time I'd felt so tired.

My eyes felt so heavy, and the world grew hazy as the aftermath of the most amazing sex of my life settled over me. I needed to sleep, just for a few hours

"Kora."

My eyes snapped open, suddenly wide awake. "Master?"

He grinned down at me, one of his massive hands coming down to stroke my hair as his dick stood to attention an inch from my nose. "Patience Kora, the night's still young, and I have a lot to teach you about Serving the Senator…"

*The End*

# Don't forget to Keep in Touch

You can find the Lord of Lust on **Facebook**, **Twitter**, **Instagram**, **Goodreads** and **Bookbud**. He loves chatting with his readers and 100% approves of stalking.

Be Sure to join his **Reader Group**, The Sweet Temptations - https://www.facebook.com/groups/580219985516975

Check out his **Website** – lmmountford.com, to learn more about his books, upcoming releases, and public appearances. And while there, don't forget to subscribe to his **Newsletter**, where you will receive a free book daily from best sellers and newbie authors alike!

# ALSO BY
# L.M. MOUNTFORD

**Age is just a number, and this collection of sinfully steamy age-gap romances will prove it...**

The Lord of lust has done it again and in this anything but sweet, four book Box Set, full of forbidden Silver Foxes and sassy Cougars, he proves that age is no boundary to love, or lust.

DELICIOUSLY SINFUL

*Liaisons*

A COLLECTION OF HOT AND ORGASMIC STORIES
FROM THE LORD OF LUST

L.M. MOUNTFORD

A collection of hot and orgasmic stories by The Lord of Lust
Do you love hard men, strong women, sizzling chemistry and
erotic scenes that make Fifty Shades of Grey look like five shades
of beige?
Well, here you go...
7 Books, 7 hard and rugged men, 7 sizzling page turners
that will have you devouring every word from start to
finish...

**Temptation has never been so sweet...**

Richard Martin's life was only just starting to come back together, then **she** opened the door in that damn little black robe that shows off plenty of leg, and every curve.

She, Rebecca Blaire, the girl from downstairs. His babysitter. She's everyman's fantasy, a big doe-eyed nymph, as beautiful as she is innocent.

Forbidden fruit in every sense of the word.

And she desperately needs his help, before her abusive father comes home and beats her black and blue.

Richard knew he should just walk away. It wasn't any of his business really, and nothing good could come from going through that door, but then...

**Some temptations are just too sweet to resist.**

He thought his temptations were over, but they were only just beginning…

Until last week, Richard Martin was just another middle-aged guy. Married to a wife he loved, father to a son he adored, stuck in a dead-end job, just counting the days go by…

Then everything changed.

He made a mistake.

Now to save his marriage, he's going to have to pay the price.

There's just one problem, Scarlet Holmes.

His Supervisor.

She loves to play games with her staff and now, seeming very aware of his little secret, she wants to play a game.

And she always gets what she wants.

Because she just so happens to be The Boss's Daughter.

Temptation at its Sweetest…
*Book 1: The Babysitter*
*Book 2: The Boss's Daughter*

Sweet Temptations: books 1&2 are sizzling tales that break all the rules and combine lust, seduction and temptation. Loaded with drama and heat, this boxset will ignite your ereader and leave you panting for more.

To all the rest of the world, Elizabeth Clarke has it all.
A successful husband. A beautiful home. And now a son
off to university. She is a perfect housewife with the perfect
life.

It's a lie.

Her husband is a lying, drinking philanderer who hates her
as much as she loathes him. Her home is beautiful, but
empty, nothing more than a gilded cage to keep her trapped
in a world she never wanted.

That is, until he came back into town.

Hugh Becket.

Her son's best friend. He's hot, young, and so forbidden.
Elizabeth knows she should stay away, but when the devil
comes knocking on her door in the middle of the night,
what's a poor neglected trophy wife to do?

**THE LORD OF LUST**
**L.M. MOUNTFORD**

*I know it's wrong to want my best friend's dad… but what about when his wife offers to share?*
Tracey has known the Burtons practically all her life.
They're her best friend's parents.
When she was a little girl they took her on days out to the beach. But she's a woman now, and they have some very important lessons to teach her…

When Mina returns for her stepbrother's 21st birthday, she thinks her days of lusting after him are over. Caught up in the heat and passion of the moment, she is stunned to find them back in bed together; their feelings clearly far from resolved. Haunted by her desire, Mina now has another problem... she must head down a path of lust and desire; torn between the dark delights of the handsome bad boy down the street and her adorable stepbrother who has always been there for her. Can she confront the truth she has long tried to bury? How far will she go to save the one she wants, but knows she can never truly have?

As an underworld princess, daughter to the boss of mob bosses all along the east coast, Sophie's life was a gilded cage. A prison of gold and silk...

That is until Luke stepped into her life.

A scrapper from the back streets, who had risen from among the ranks to stand in her shadow.

Luke, her bodyguard, and her secret lover.

Their destinies were never meant to cross, but they had. It was impossible, forbidden, but they couldn't resist...

Now their one reckless night has become a desperate fight for their lives.

*I may have been a bad influence on her when we were kids, but this new side of her is going to ruin me...*

They were the best of friends. Then they shared a night of passion and in the morning she was gone and Alex has spent years trying to move on.

But then an email arrives out of the blue and suddenly he finds himself boarding the first plane bound for Australia with nothing but his passport and an overnight bag. He's no idea what he'll do, or he's going to say, but one thing's for sure...

He's not going home without her.

*Together in Sydney is a Second Chance Romance full of steamy scenes and bad language. It's only recommended for readers 18+. No cliffhanger. Guaranteed HEA!*

An erotic PNR/Vampire story by
*J.A. Howard*

*Blood*
**Lust**

The Thirst always
*wins...*

Sooner or later, the thirst always wins...
After a thousand years, Lucian had given up any interest in
the world. His only concern that night was finding his next
drink, preferably from a flavoursome twenty-something with
loose morals and no expectations. Then he saw her...
Kate is just a girl from the country, who came to the city with
her brother to find a life away from their parents' car crash.
That is until the police came knocking on her door one
morning and ripped her new life apart.
Now she has nothing and no one, with only one on her
mind...
When these worlds collide, and the things that go bump in
the night come calling, can these two mend the rifts in each
other and give them what they need?

'I'm sorry Cassy, but you're just too boring for me,'
That was the story of Cassandra's life.
She was always that girl. The curvy plain jane. She was fine
with it, right up until her hot bad boy ex threw it in her face
before walking out of her life. Leaving her depressed and
reeling, doubting everything about herself and her future...
So her best friend has spirited her away to her family's
Gibraltar Vila for a little fun in the sun, some much needed
girl time, and a whole lot of boys.
There's just one problem.
David, her best friend's recently divorced dad also
happens to be staying at the villa. And he's no boy...

Vickey Romano is the girl with a secret you don't want to
bring home to mum.

Beautiful, haunted, and on the run, she works a string of
temp jobs and never lets anyone get too close. Until that is,
she meets Jake. The living definition of dark and dangerous,
he tells her nothing about himself, keeps a SIG P226 in his
bedside table and can make her go weak-kneed with just a
word.

She knows she should stay away, he has her caught in his
web and she's helpless to resist.

All she can do is hope her past doesn't kill him in the
process...

*Broken is a hard and gritty Dark romance. The opening in the
Broken Heart Series, it balances sex and violence on a knife edge
and will draw you down a web of mystery with every page.*

They were the very poster children for the boy and girl
next door, if a couple of streets apart.
Friends for longer than forever. They'd walked to school
together. He'd protected her from the bullies when they
teased her about her glasses. She'd tended to his cuts and
bruises when he fell. He pushed her to try new things. She
snuck looks at him when he wasn't looking.
All her life, Faye had loved Terry, but he was oblivious. He's
her best friend, her closest friend, but he's oblivious and now
he has a Girlfriend. All day long, she has to watch them
together and it's killing her. She wants him, all of him, but
he's taken. So, instead, she wants one night. Just once, one
night, between friends.
One night, just once...